Sea Transport

Carmel Reilly

Contents

Sea Transport

From One Part of the World to Another

Every day, people buy and use things that come from faraway places. Computers, clothing, toys, cars and many kinds of food come from overseas. But how do all of these goods get from one part of the world to another?

While planes can carry some goods between countries, most items are transported by sea in large ships called **cargo** ships. Different kinds of cargo ships carry different kinds of products (things made to be sold). There are **tankers** and **bulk carriers** to take large amounts of liquid or dry goods, refrigerated ships to transport cold products and ships that only carry vehicles. The most common type of cargo ship is the container ship, which can transport many kinds of items in large **containers**.

a container ship

a tanker

There are thousands of cargo ships at sea. They are constantly on the move, sailing between **ports** all over the world to pick up and drop off goods. Their ability to transport products easily and cheaply is what makes sea transport so popular.

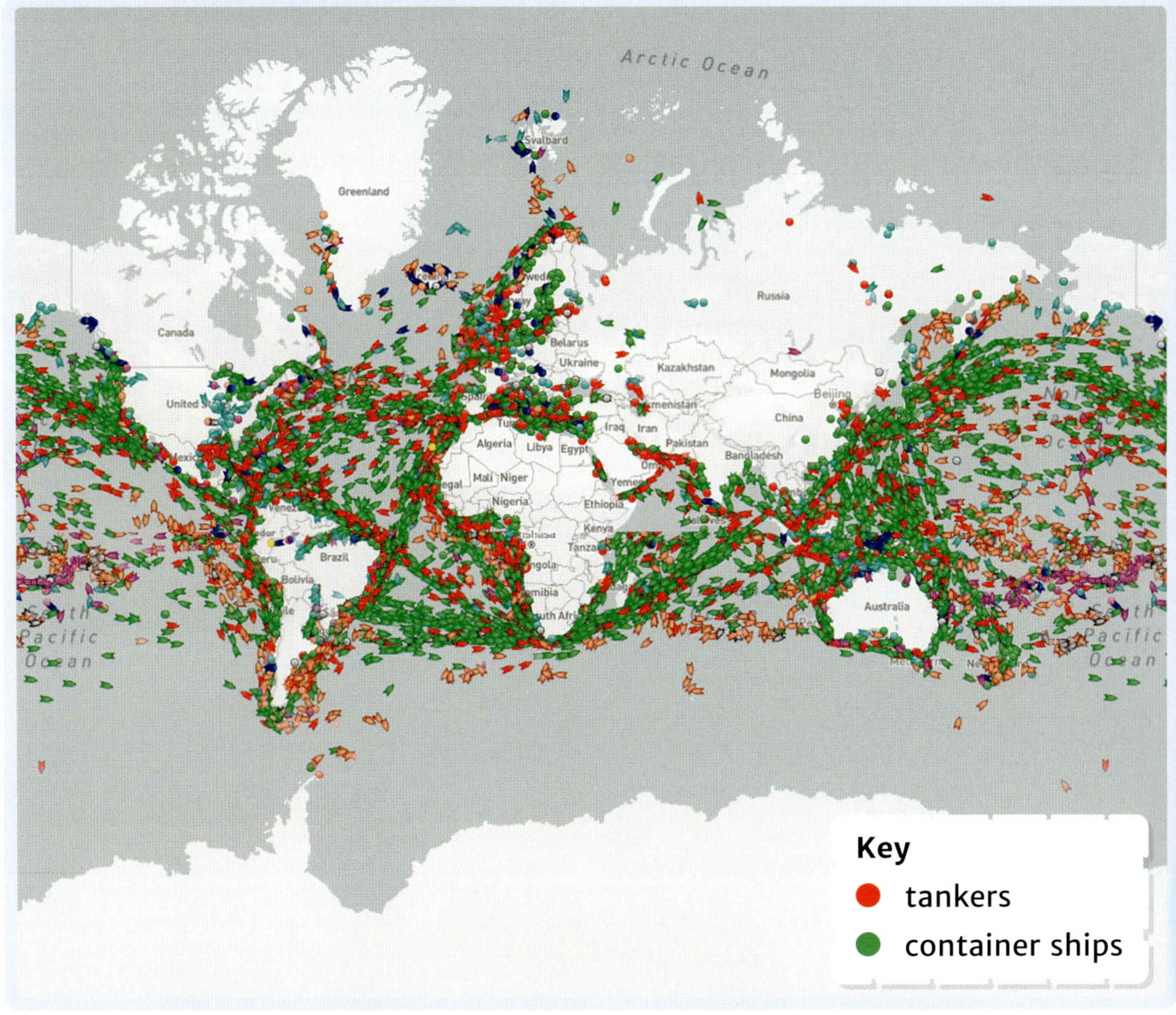

This map shows every ship on the ocean at one time.

Ships and Their Cargo

Cargo ships carry almost 90 per cent of the goods that are sent around the world. The most common types of cargo are food, vehicles, furniture, electronics, minerals, iron and steel, clothes and toys. Most cargo is sent between companies from different countries, while a small part of cargo is made up of things that people have ordered online.

With so many different kinds of cargo, many different kinds of ships are needed to carry it.

The Different Parts of a Container Ship

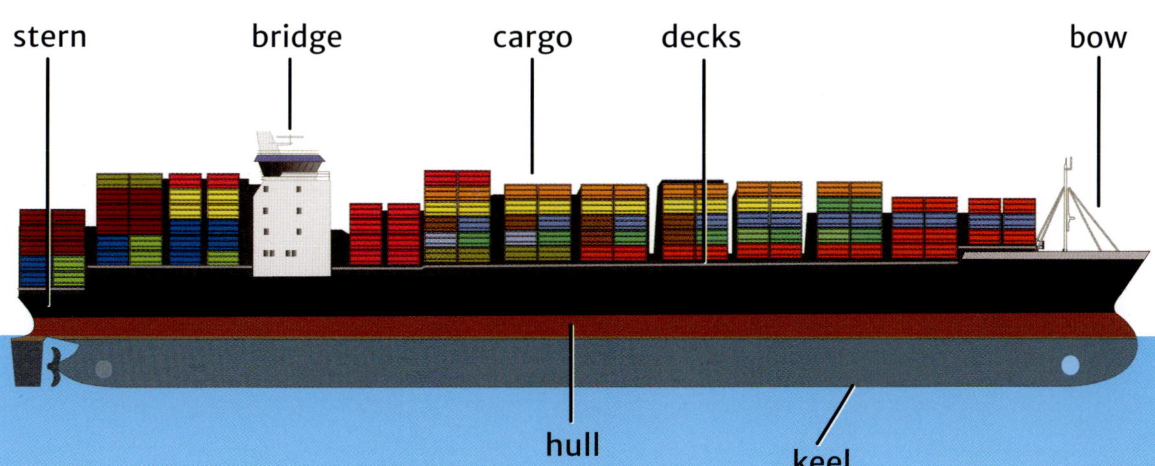

Tankers and Bulk Carriers

Tankers and bulk carriers are ships that carry large amounts of unpackaged goods. Tankers can transport liquids, such as chemicals and oil, or gases. Bulk carriers transport dry goods, such as grain or woodchips. The products these ships carry are loaded directly into the **hold**, which is a large space in the ship's **hull**, or base. In many cases, these ships have been made to transport only one thing, such as **petroleum** or fruit juice, and they will only ever carry that product.

Grain is loaded into the hold of a bulk carrier in Ukraine.

Roll-on Roll-off Ships

There are some cargo ships that are only used to transport vehicles. These are called **roll-on roll-off ships**. They were given this name because vehicles can be driven straight on and off them at a **dock**. These ships can carry cars, trucks, tractors and even heavy machinery, such as bulldozers and cranes.

Brand new cars are lined up to be driven onto a roll-on roll-off ship.

Roll-on roll-off ships have wide hulls with a number of **decks**, or levels. These allow them to fit in as many vehicles as possible. The largest ships have 12 decks, and can carry more than 6000 cars at one time.

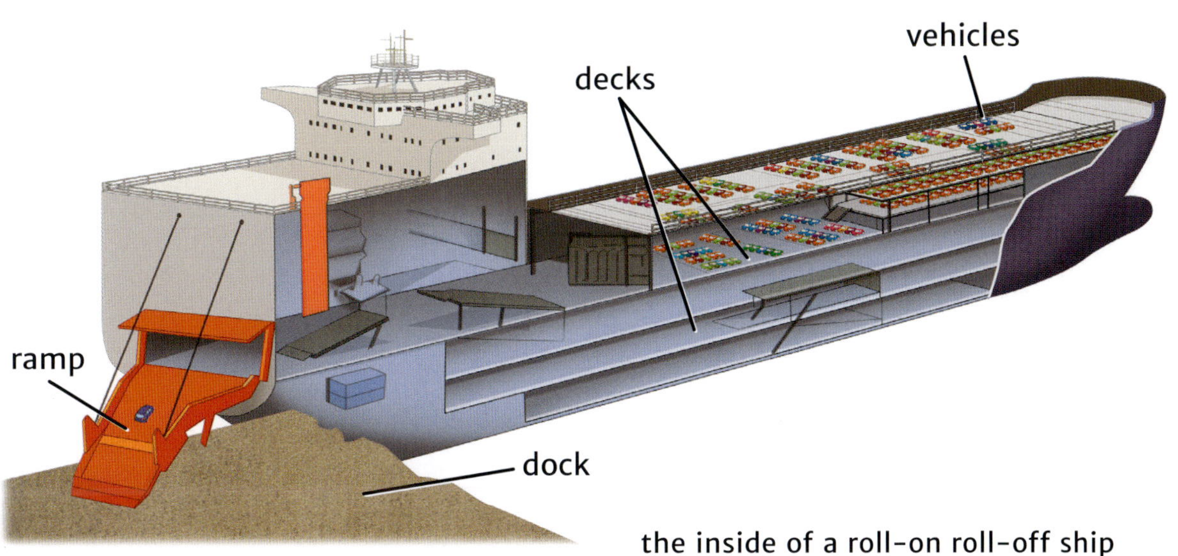

the inside of a roll-on roll-off ship

Refrigerated Ships

Refrigerated ships are made to transport goods that need to be kept cold. These goods include fruit and vegetables, meat and dairy products and medical supplies. On some refrigerated ships, the products are packed directly into one large, refrigerated hold, and everything is stored at the same temperature. On others, different goods are put into separate refrigerated containers. Each container has its own temperature setting. This allows some products to be kept colder than others.

A worker stacks boxes of bananas on a refrigerated ship.

Container Ships

Most ocean cargo travels on container ships. These are **vessels** that carry a wide range of small- and medium-sized goods in huge metal boxes known as containers.

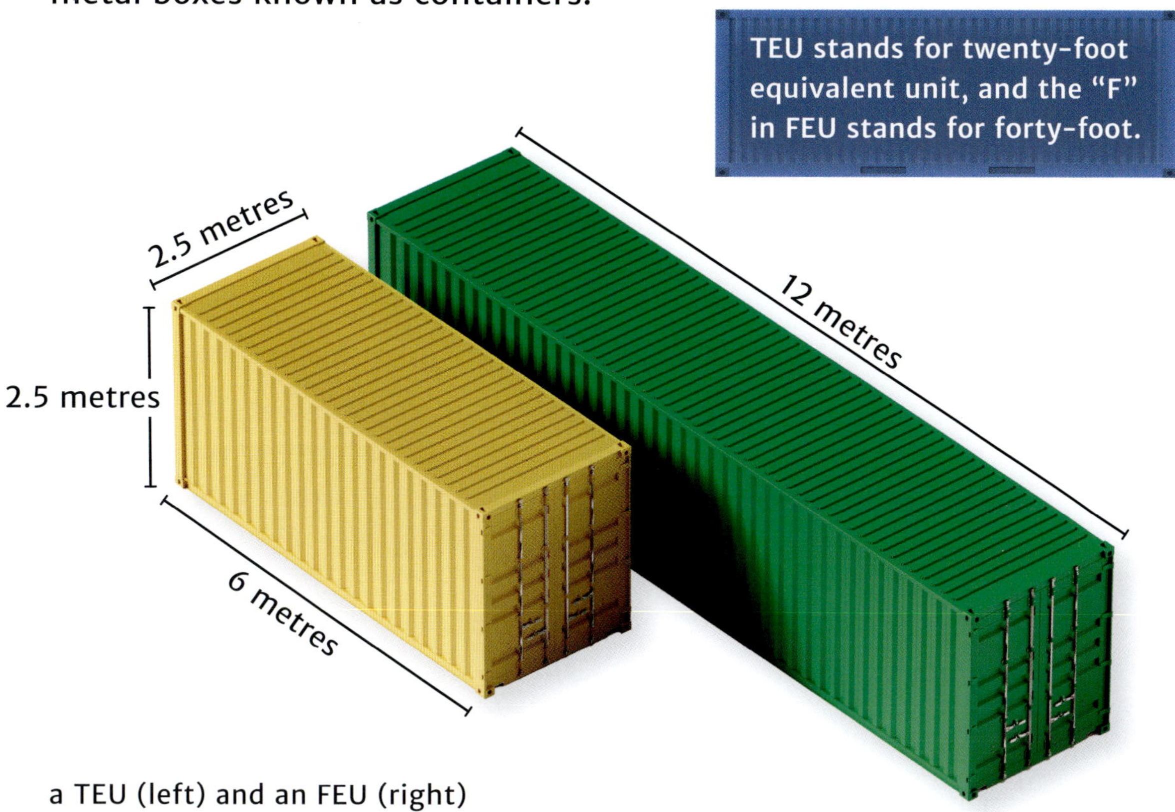

a TEU (left) and an FEU (right)

Containers come in standard (TEU) and large (FEU) sizes. A TEU container is able to hold up to 48 000 bananas, 24 000 cans of food or 6000 shoe boxes. An FEU container is twice as long as a TEU container and holds twice as much.

A crane loads containers one by one at a port in Germany.

Containers are stacked by cranes, one on top of another, onto the decks of container ships. Containers also fit neatly onto the back of trucks. This means they can be easily transported to and from ports.

Super Container Ships

The biggest container ships are known as superships. They are about 400 metres long and 60 metres wide, or the size of 4 soccer fields placed end to end. They are able to carry over 20 000 TEU containers. When a supership is loaded with containers, it can be as tall as a six-storey building. These ships are so enormous that it is difficult for them to sail in some places, such as narrow or shallow **canals**. They are only able to be loaded and unloaded in a few ports. Most ports are not big or deep enough to fit these superships.

How Big Is a Supership?

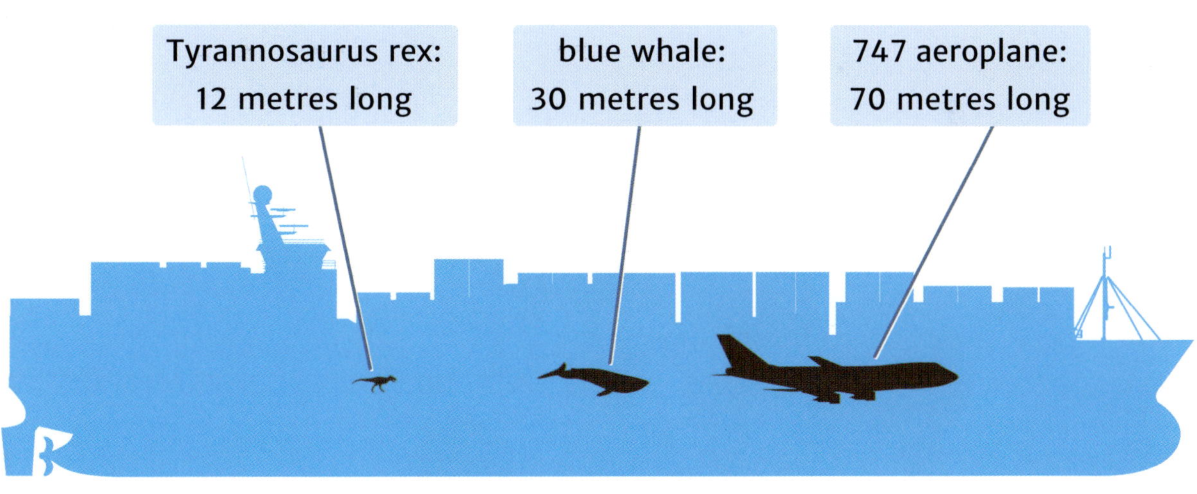

Out on the Ocean

Shipping Lanes

At any one time, there are thousands of cargo ships sailing on the ocean. They are constantly travelling between ports, along what are known as shipping lanes. Shipping lanes are routes or paths that have been followed for many years. They help ships avoid dangerous coastlines and uneven **seabeds**, which can cause ships to have accidents or **run aground**. These lanes also make the most of fast-flowing currents and strong winds to provide the fastest and safest sea journeys.

There are thousands of shipping lanes around the world. However, with more and more sea traffic, some of them have become very busy.

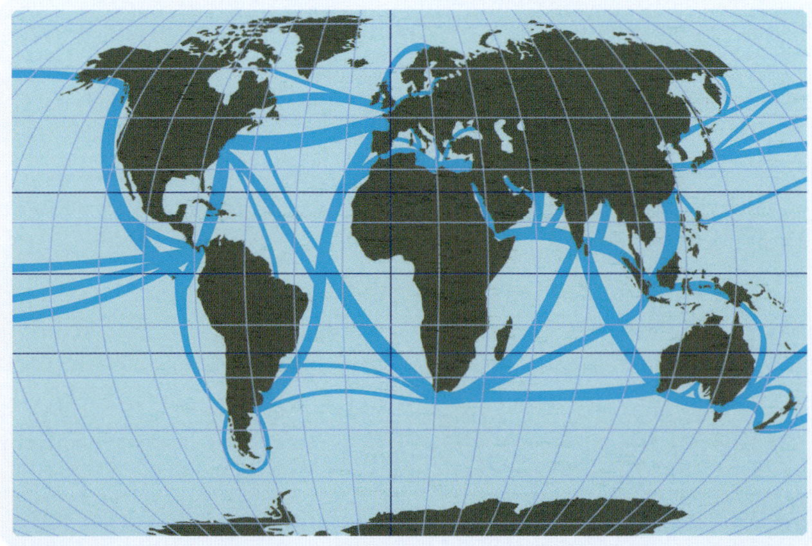

The blue lines on the map show the most common shipping lanes around the world.

Ports

There are more than 800 cargo ports along the world's coastlines. Some of these ports are very large, while others are quite small. Many ports take general cargo and containers. However, some are special ports that only receive certain goods such as grain, minerals or petroleum.

Docks are places within ports where ships pull up to have their cargo loaded or unloaded.

The largest and busiest cargo port in the world is in Shanghai, China. In 2019, 43.6 million TEU containers and 542.5 million tonnes of cargo were loaded and unloaded at its docks.

Loading and Unloading

In the world's most advanced ports, computers and machines do most of the work. First, computer programs work out how best to stack the containers. Driverless trucks then transport the containers from a waiting area to the docks.

A container is loaded onto a driverless truck.

Finally, computer-operated cranes lift the containers onto the ships. When they are loaded, a team of people goes onto the ship. They check that the containers are safe, and that the containers cannot open or move around on their journey.

Cranes are used to load containers onto the ships.

Once a ship is loaded, it begins its journey. Some ships sail directly to distant ports, where they deliver all their cargo. Other ships drop containers off at a number of ports along the route.

At a port, the containers are unloaded by cranes, placed on port trucks and taken to a storage area on the docks. Later, the containers are picked up by road trucks and delivered to a shipping company. The company then passes them on to the buyer.

A huge container ship sets sail.

The Dangers of Transporting Goods by Sea

Storms and Accidents

Storms at sea are always a danger for ships. Modern ships are strong and well-made, so they rarely sink. However, ships are carrying bigger loads than ever before, and extreme weather is becoming more common. When vessels are caught in wild storms, they can sometimes tip and lose some of their cargo from the top decks.

Every year, thousands of containers fall or are washed overboard. Occasionally, an accident on board a ship or a problem with **inflammable** cargo can cause a ship to explode or catch fire.

shipping containers that have fallen off a cargo ship

Reefs, Shallow Waters and Narrow Channels

Some ships have hit reefs or have become stuck in shallow waters or narrow **channels**. Sometimes, these events can cause ships to tip and lose their cargo. At other times, ships are able to be rescued and towed away by tugboats. However, the time it takes to rescue vessels adds to the cost of transport, which makes the goods more expensive for the buyer.

This container ship ran aground in shallow waters at Church Bay, UK.

Pirates

Pirates are people who board ships to steal cargo. Sometimes pirates open containers and take valuable goods like phones and computers. At other times, they will steal a whole ship, such as a tanker that is carrying a useful product like petroleum.

Shipping and the Environment

Sea shipping is a more **energy-efficient** way to transport goods than transporting by plane. This is because ships are able to carry larger loads while using less fuel and creating less pollution. However, in recent times, demand for overseas goods has increased enormously, so there are now thousands more cargo ships sailing the oceans. More ships means that there is more water, air and soil pollution.

Grams of Carbon Emissions per Tonne-Kilometre

For every 1 km travelled, cargo ships release much less CO2 than trucks or air freight.

container ship	oil tanker	bulk carrier	truck	air freight
3 g	6 g	8 g	80 g	435 g

Water Pollution

Pollution is also caused by ships losing their cargo at sea. During accidents or storms, things such as plastic, poisonous chemicals, oil and food can be swept into the water. In an emergency, ships sometimes release the fuel they have on board, in order to prevent fires. All of these substances can pollute both underwater environments and nearby shores, causing long-lasting damage.

In 2021, containers of chia seeds spilled into the ocean near the west coast of the USA. The seeds formed a **sludge** that washed up onto the shore, causing a threat to the snowy plover birds that were nesting there.

It is clear that there are some problems with sea transport. However, on the whole, transporting goods by sea is the safest, easiest and cheapest way to move things from one part of the world to another.

Stuck in the Suez Canal

The *Ever Given* is a super container ship owned by a company called Evergreen. It was built in 2018 and is one of 85 ships in the world that can carry 20 000 or more TEU containers.

In March 2021, the ship was travelling from Asia to Europe when it ran aground in the Suez Canal in Egypt. The *Ever Given* and its cargo blocked the long canal, causing worldwide shipping delays until it was finally freed six days later.

Length: 399.9 metres

Width of hull: 58.8 metres

Containers on board: about 18 000

Crew on board: 25

The *Ever Given*'s cargo included lemons, vegetables, tofu, computer products, furniture, electronics, barbecues, sun lounges, swimwear, lawnmowers and camping equipment.

Entering the Suez Canal

The *Ever Given* entered the Suez Canal on 23 March 2021. Two weeks before, the ship had left Malaysia, loaded with about 18 000 containers, and was on its way to the Netherlands. It was part of a line of vessels making their way slowly along the Suez Canal in difficult conditions. Strong winds gusted off the Egyptian desert, creating a dust storm that made it hard to see, and hard to steer.

The Suez Canal is a human-made canal that is 200 metres wide and 193 kilometres long, running through Egypt to connect the Mediterranean Sea and the Red Sea.

A line of ships sails down the Suez Canal on a clear day.

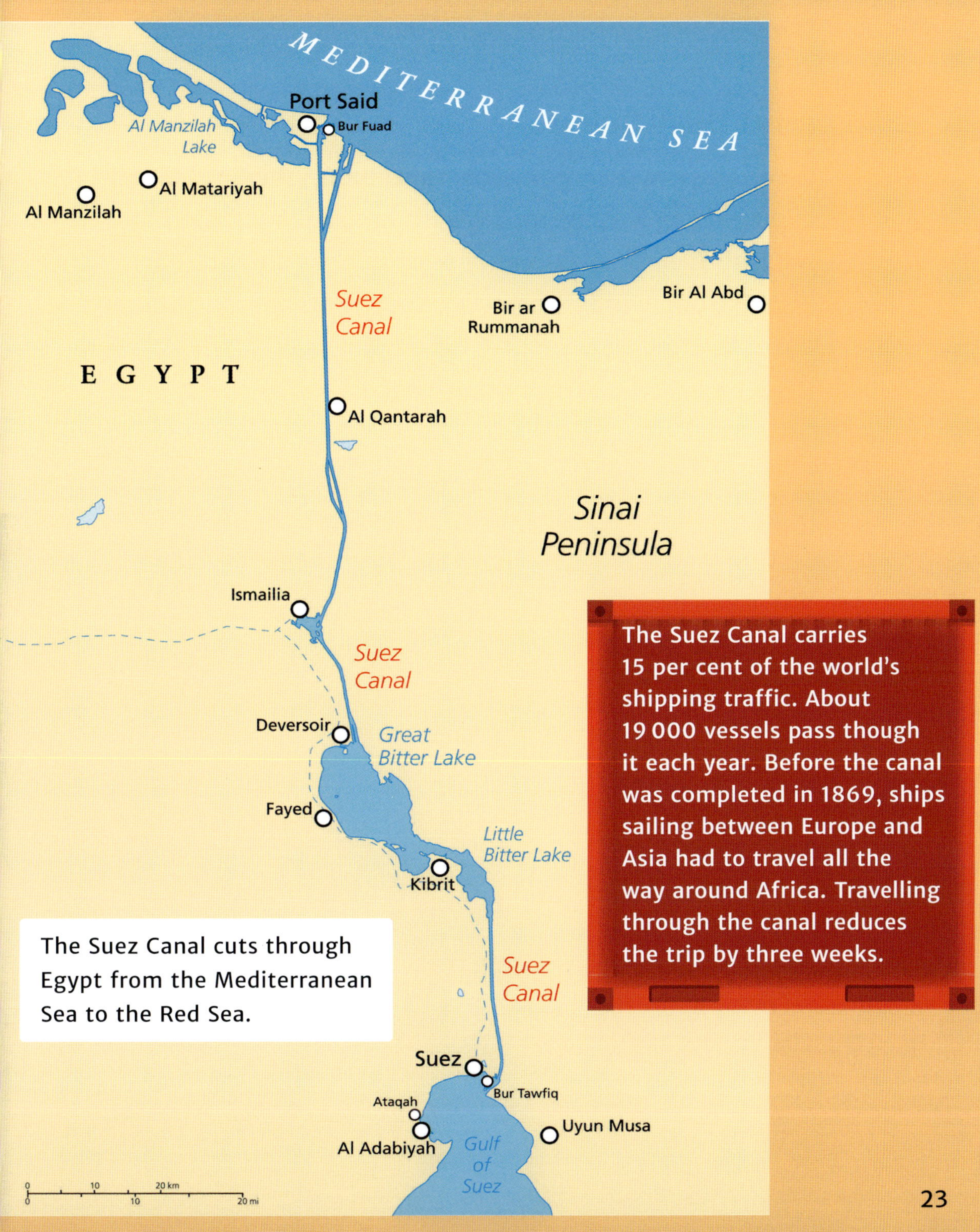

The Suez Canal cuts through Egypt from the Mediterranean Sea to the Red Sea.

The Suez Canal carries 15 per cent of the world's shipping traffic. About 19 000 vessels pass though it each year. Before the canal was completed in 1869, ships sailing between Europe and Asia had to travel all the way around Africa. Travelling through the canal reduces the trip by three weeks.

A Powerful Dust Storm

It takes between 12 and 16 hours to travel along the Suez Canal, and the trip that day was even slower than usual because of a dust storm. The *Ever Given* had only been in the canal for about 2 hours when strong winds started to drive it off course. The tall load on board seemed to act a little like a sail, helping the wind to push the ship from left to right and back.

A dust storm blows across the Suez Canal.

The ship sped up in an attempt to correct its course, but it kept twisting further to the right until its **bow**, or front, hit one side of the canal. At the same time, the **stern**, or back, swung around to the left and wedged itself on the opposite bank. In a matter of minutes, the ship had run aground and was stuck.

The bow and the stern of the *Ever Given* became stuck in the shallow banks of the canal.

A Bigger Problem

Not only had the *Ever Given* run aground, it was also wedged right across the canal, blocking the path for other ships. This meant the ships that had already entered the canal were also stuck, because they could not move forward or backward. All those ships had products on board that needed to be delivered. The *Ever Given* itself had close to a billion dollars' worth of goods on board that people were waiting for in the Netherlands.

As the days went by, more and more ships became backed up at both ends of the canal, unable to enter, until there were over 400 ships waiting.

Cargo ships were waiting to enter the blocked Suez Canal.

A bulldozer was sent in to clear sand and rocks from the bank where the ship's bow was stuck. At the same time, local tugboats attached ropes to one side of the ship and attempted to pull it around. Neither of these actions had any effect on the huge ship.

If the *Ever Given* could have been unloaded, that might have helped it become unstuck from the bank. However, there was no equipment available in the canal to lift the huge containers.

Authorities used a bulldozer to try to dig some of the sand and rocks from the canal to free the *Ever Given*.

Help from Outside

A few days later, two giant tugboats from the Netherlands and Italy reached the *Ever Given*. They had managed to make their way along the canal from the Mediterranean Sea, edging past all the other vessels. The two tugboats worked together, using enormous ropes. Two days later, they were finally able to pull the ship away from the bank.

After being stuck for almost a week, the *Ever Given* was finally free.

Authorities used giant tugboats to pull the *Ever Given* with heavy ropes.

The *Ever Given* was able to sail down the canal with help from the tugboats.

Getting Back to Normal

Once the *Ever Given* had been moved, the cargo ships that were waiting in and around the Suez Canal were also able to continue their journeys. However, the delay badly affected sea transport. Many ports in Europe and Asia had become crowded with goods. This was because the ships that had been stuck in the canal were not able to pick up or drop off cargo. It took two months for ports to be cleared, and the delivery of goods was delayed in many countries.

The *Ever Given*'s accident made people realise how one small blockage in a sea route could affect the whole world.

Glossary

bow (*noun*)	the front of a ship or boat
bulk carriers (*noun*)	ships that can carry large amounts of dry goods
canals (*noun*)	waterways made by humans to let ships cross through land
cargo (*noun*)	items carried on a ship, plane, train or truck
channels (*noun*)	long trenches filled with water
containers (*noun*)	large metal boxes to hold things that are carried on a ship
decks (*noun*)	the floors or levels of a ship
dock (*noun*)	a place in the water where ships can stop to be loaded and unloaded
energy-efficient (*adjective*)	making good use of energy, such as fuel or electricity
hold (*noun*)	the space in a ship for carrying goods

hull (*noun*) the main part or body of a ship

inflammable (*adjective*) easy to set on fire

petroleum (*noun*) a liquid that is used to make fuel and oil

ports (*noun*) towns or cities where ships can stop

roll-on roll-off ships (*noun*) boats that allow vehicles to drive on and off

run aground (*verb*) to touch the ground with the bottom of a boat or ship when in shallow water

seabeds (*noun*) the floors of the ocean

sludge (*noun*) a thick liquid or mud

stern (*noun*) the back of a ship or boat

tankers (*noun*) ships that can carry large amounts of liquids

vessels (*noun*) ships or boats

Index